My grandchildren loved Jo Duhn's first Casey and the Crab, The Gruesome Green Goo! We just finished reading her second book and now they are hooked! Casey and the Crab 2, Trinidad Tomayo's Treasure is filled with adventure and excitement that will capture even the most reluctant reader's attention! Great job!

Robbee Kubischta
Westminster, Colorado

****

With a wonderful sense of humor and adventure, Jo Duhn introduces her second Casey and the Crab. Her positive view of life paired with ecological good sense and love of learning contribute to a tale that is attractive and entertaining.

Bettie Ogren
Livingston, Texas

****

Jo Duhn has proven that her first book was just the beginning! This has as much, if not more, excitement and adventure as her first Casey and the Crab. My grandchildren couldn't put it down and neither could I. We can't wait for the third one!!

Rick Howard
Huntington, IN

****

Jo Duhn has done it again! Casey and Cap go on another island adventure looking for pirate treasure. Full of suspense and action!

Charlie & Sylvia Simmonds
Ontario, Canada

CASEY & the Crab II

Antonio,
Read, write and learn
something new every day.
You are AMAZING!

JoDe

Jo Duhn's

CASEY & the Crab II

TRINIDAD TOMAYO'S TREASURE

TATE PUBLISHING
AND ENTERPRISES, LLC

Published by Tate Publishing & Enterprises, LLC
127 E. Trade Center Terrace | Mustang, Oklahoma 73064 USA
1.888.361.9473 | www.tatepublishing.com

Tate Publishing is committed to excellence in the publishing industry. The company reflects the philosophy established by the founders, based on Psalm 68:11,
"The Lord gave the word and great was the company of those who published it."

Book design copyright © 2012 by Tate Publishing, LLC. All rights reserved.
Cover design by Rodrigo Adolfo
Interior design by Caypeeline Casas

Published in the United States of America

ISBN: 978-1-62147-266-7
1. Juvenile Fiction / Action & Adventure / Pirates
2. Juvenile Fiction / Mysteries & Detective Stories
12.08.14

Dedication

My love to Dick for his support. And, as always, thanks Sarah H.

Chapter 1

October, 1748: the eighty-four-foot brigantine *Dragon's Fire* tried to make it to the safety of Laguna De Oro, a narrow bay sheltered by a barrier island, as the storm blew in from the south. Laguna De Oro was well known to sailors and pirates alike and had saved many ships and their crew from sinking in the violent storms that came up suddenly at this time of year. The large, twin-masted pirate ship was armed with ten canons and a forty-man crew who now struggled with the square mainsail that was being torn to shreds by the fierce winds. Although it was nearly noon, the day was as dark as any night the captain had ever seen.

Captain Trinadad Tomayo stood on the upper deck, screaming orders to the men, but his words were carried away, and he could not be heard above the howl of the wind. The rain that pelted him stung like needle pricks and made the deck as slippery as ice. Above the howl of the wind, he heard a sickening sound and watched in horror as the mast for the mainsail snapped and crashed to the deck.

Men were screaming in fear and pain, and still the wind continued on its destructive path. Without the mainsail, the ship floundered for a few moments, and then, turning sideways to the wind, powerful waves pushed it on to a sandbar, and it began to tip.

Running back to his quarters, the captain grabbed two of his men and told them to follow him. Inside, he commanded his men to bring a heavy chest to one of the small landing boats that was still attached to the ship. The ship was doomed, but maybe the treasure could still be saved. Before leaving his quarters, he turned and took one last look at what had become his home. His eyes landed on a small leather-bound book that he had left on his cot. This was his personal journal, the story of his life as a pirate. In this book he had documented his defeats and his conquests. Quickly wrapping the book in a piece of oiled leather to protect it from the rain, he stuck it into his shirt and left the room.

As the men struggled on the now severely angled deck, the captain could hear cracking sounds above the screaming wind as the hull of the huge ship began to break apart. He screamed for the men to abandon ship, but even as he gave the orders, he knew it was too late. As he boarded the landing boat weighted down now with a chest full of stolen treasure, he doubted his own chances of making it to land in these heavy seas.

After twenty-eight hours the storm passed, and the sun rose on a clear and bright day. Trinadad Tomayo, once the captain of his own ship and a crew of fierce but loyal pirates, found himself alone on a small island. He was still clinging to the landing boat that was now mostly buried in the sand. There was no sign of either his ship or his crew anywhere, and the only sounds he heard were the pounding of the waves and the incessant cries of the seagulls. The chest, filled with stolen gold, silver, and jewels, was still in the boat, and it, too, was mostly buried in the sand.

It took him three days to drag the heavy chest to the middle of the island and bury it. The large puddles of fresh water that had collected during the heavy rain had mostly dried up the first day, leaving only stagnant pools of brackish water. Swarms of mosquitoes came out, and Captain Tomayo found himself weak from hunger and thirst and being eaten up by the voracious insects. He began to hallucinate.

Indians from across the bay visited the island regularly by canoe to hunt the large jack rabbits and to fish from the sandy beaches. Whenever he saw them coming, Tomayo would hide in the tall grass and wait for them to leave. It was commonly believed that these extremely tall Indians were cannibals. This was not true, but even if it was they would not have eaten Tomayo. He was obviously sick, delirious with fever, and they did not want to risk getting too close. Keeping their distance, they watched him. On day five, they observed him on a high sand dune sitting right next to one of the giant blue crabs that populated the island. He talked and ranted at great length, and the Indians joked that the big crab looked almost like it was participating in the conversation. Yes, Captain Tomayo was obviously very sick, and these Indians knew better than to get too close to a white man with a fever.

On day ten, Captain Trinadad Tomayo was rescued by the crew of the Spanish galleon *Santa Antonita*. He was promptly thrown into chains and held in the hold of the ship where he would stay for the next two months while they returned to Spain. There, he was to be tried as a thief and a pirate of the high seas.

Chapter 2

Present Day

Casey looked around the room and marveled once again. Sometimes it was still hard for him to believe that this wasn't a dream. He was sitting in a little diner with his good friend, Cap. But this wasn't just any diner, and Cap wasn't just any friend. Cap was a crab, a real, honest-to-goodness, giant blue crab and the constable of the crab village below the sand where this diner was.

Casey met Cap on a misty, rainy first day of spring break pretty much by accident. All of his friends were off on various vacations with their families, and Casey had sort of been feeling sorry for himself, mostly because he had to clean his room that day. By the time he was done, it was rainy, and the tide was out. That meant no surfing, the only thing he really loved to do. Sitting on a sand dune, staring out across the beach to the ocean, Casey had been startled by a voice. Looking around, he saw no one, only a crab, the biggest, bluest crab he had ever seen in his life!

Thinking that he was dreaming, Casey had followed the crab right through a hidden tunnel, where the sight of the crab's little town shocked him. There was a park, beautifully landscaped with sea grass and crisscrossed with sand walkways. Beyond the park were neat little houses decorated with shells in every color and shape and buildings constructed with wood and materials salvaged from long ago ship wrecks. Casey had lived his entire life on this island with his parents and never dreamed such a place existed.

As a human, he was not welcome at first. In fact, the crabs here were very angry with him, and every other human as well, because of the actions of a few men. These men had been pouring toxic waste down the drains at an abandoned plant, and the crabs were getting very sick. Delores, Cap's daughter and the owner of the diner, was especially hostile to Casey. She pretty much hated all humans and didn't want Casey anywhere near the crab village, especially after her son, little Mickey, got sick.

All of that changed after Casey and Cap joined forces to expose the polluters and save the village and possibly the entire island. He and Cap had become very good friends and saw each other almost every day either on the beach or here, in the crab village.

So now, sitting here looking down through the glass of an old porthole that served as a table, Casey was amazed again. The brass on the porthole gleamed like gold, and it was hard to believe that it had been salvaged from a ship wreck long ago. There were several of these tables in this little diner, and a long counter of dark, polished wood separated the dining area from the little kitchen in the back. The smell of cinnamon and coffee filled the air.

He was the only human allowed in the crab's village and had been sworn to secrecy. Of course, he wouldn't have told anyone anyway. After all, who would believe that there were talking crabs living below the sand? Or that they had an entire village complete with things like a bakery, a diner, and a police station?

"King me!" Cap yelled, moving a piece across the checker board.

"Ah, Cap," Casey said with a laugh, "I don't know why I play checkers with you. You always win!"

"Ha!" Cap exclaimed. "Maybe it's just crab luck!"

Casey laughed good-naturedly and, picking up his mug, took a long last gulp of Kelp Kola. He remembered the first time he had ever tried it. Delores had slammed the mugs down so hard he thought the table would break. It was milky brown with greenish foam on top, and Casey wasn't sure it was OK to drink. He wouldn't have even tried it, but all the crabs in the diner were watching him closely. He didn't want to insult anyone; they were mad enough that he was there. After trying it, he understood why it was Cap's favorite. It tasted like chocolate-flavored root beer, and it was delicious!

"I've got to go, Cap," Casey said. "My parents are going out tonight so mom is fixing my dinner early, and I better not be late." He gave a little wave to Delores and then turned back to Cap. "I'll see you tomorrow."

"Maybe then I'll beat you at chess," Cap said with a smile.

After crossing the park, Casey made sure no one was around and then crawled out of the well-hidden tunnel on his hands and knees. It was late afternoon, but there were still a lot of people on the beach taking advantage of the gentle breeze that floated in from the ocean. He could hear the squawking of the seagulls and smell burgers frying at the Beach Comber Café, a popular burger stand right on the beach. Making his way to the public pavilion, Casey crossed the parking lot and ran the half block to his home.

Chapter 3

"Casey, are you listening? This is serious, and if you aren't going to pay attention then your mom and I will just have to stay home tonight."

"I'm sorry, Dad. I'm listening. You'll have your cell phone with you, and I know you're the first button on speed dial."

"I'm sorry, too, but I'm very worried. This little town has always been so safe, but since Mrs. Anderson's break-in last night, I'm not so comfortable leaving you all alone."

"Don't worry, Dad," Casey said. "I'll keep the phone with me and all the doors locked, and if anyone does decide to break into our house, I'll whack 'em with my surf board!"

"Yeah, that's pretty much what I was afraid of," his father chuckled. "Just call me, okay? If you hear anything, call me. We're only going to be two blocks away so I can be home in a minute. And don't forget, second on the speed dial is your Uncle Drew." Drew wasn't really Casey's uncle, but he was his dad's best friend and the police chief on the island.

"Don't worry! Just go and have fun, and I promise I'll call right away if I hear anything."

After his parents left, Casey checked all the doors, and then he popped a pack of popcorn in the microwave oven. He played the video games he had rented from Island Movie Rentals for a while and then turned on the scary movie that he had rented at the same time. He was planning on watching it with his best friend, Jessie, but couldn't wait. It started out okay, but it got scarier as it went on, and then he started hearing strange noises in the house. Finally, he turned the movie off and went through the house, turning on every light. He would never admit that he was scared, but he took the phone to his bedroom and crawled into bed without even brushing his teeth, promising himself that he would brush twice tomorrow morning.

Chapter 4

"So, why would anyone want to break in to Mrs. Anderson's house anyway?" Casey asked his father the next morning. "She's not rich or anything." He and his father sat at the kitchen table, each with a big bowl of Coco Puffs as the morning sun streamed in through the kitchen window. His mom would have preferred that the two of them eat a better breakfast, like fruit and yogurt, but Coco Puffs was his dad's favorite, too, so they usually had breakfast together before his dad went to work.

"They're still investigating, but Officer Drew mentioned to me that she was planning to donate her collection of books to the library soon. There was an article in the paper about it. Apparently, whoever did this had gone through every book in the collection, and then they just ransacked the house. They might have been trying to cover up something by tearing the house apart, or maybe they didn't find what they were looking for."

"What were they after?" Casey asked.

"No one really knows. But Mrs. Anderson said that she didn't think they took anything."

"I think that's just weird."

"Not if they didn't find what they were looking for. They would keep looking, and burglars usually don't take the time to be careful while they look through everything. They just keep throwing things around while they hunt for whatever they want."

"No, I mean, well...that, too," Casey said, stirring his cereal in his bowl. "But I think it's weird that Mrs. Anderson spent most of her life as the librarian here, and she collected books on the side. I mean...I like to read, but collecting books like that seems a little weird. She could just go to the library like everybody else."

"Well, the books she collected were one-of-a-kind, pretty rare books. I think that books are her passion. You'll understand when you're a little older, I suppose. So what do you have planned for today?"

"Jessie and I are going to meet up about ten and do some surfing."

"See, I think you already know about passion! Mrs. Anderson feels about books like you do about surfing. Well, have fun. I've got to get going," his father said as he put his bowl in the dishwasher. "Don't forget that it's garbage day. Be sure to get it all to the curb early, and don't forget the recycle bins this time."

"I'll do it right now, Dad."

* * *

After surfing for several hours, Casey was ready to head to the Beach Comber, the beachside burger stand, for a nice thick shake and maybe an order of fries.

"I got my allowance so I'll pay," he said to Jessie.

"I wish I could, Casey," Jessie said, twisting the salt water out of her long brown hair, "but I have to watch my little sister this afternoon. My mom's got some kind of meeting, and she wants me home with Sara, especially since Mrs. Anderson's got broken into. My mom's really freaked."

"Yeah, my mom is, too. I just feel sorry for Mrs. Anderson," Casey said, shaking his head sadly. "I liked her as a librarian a lot better than the one we have now. She would tell you all about the books and help you pick out just the right one."

"She was always happy to see you come in, too," Jessie added, "No matter how young or old you were. The new guy just acts like you're bothering him when you go in."

"Hey!" Casey said excitedly. "Let's go visit her this afternoon. She could probably use some help picking up, and I'll bet we could cheer her up."

"Casey, I told you, I have to watch Sara."

"So? We'll take Sara with us. I'll drop my board off at home and come pick you up."

"Maybe," Jessie said tentatively, "but I gotta check with my mom first. If that's okay with her, I'll call you."

Chapter 5

"Oh, my! It's Casey, Jessie, and is that little Sara? You've grown so much I hardly recognized you! How wonderful of you to visit. Come in, come in!" Mrs. Anderson opened the door wide and gestured toward the little living room just off the entry. "I have lemonade or cola, and how about some fresh oatmeal cookies? I just took them out of the oven."

The shelves that lined two walls of the living room were empty, and the floor was covered with stacks of books. The sofa was clear, but both of the high-backed chairs were piled with books, as was the coffee table. A box in the middle of the room held shards of broken vases, several broken picture frames, and a small black box with a red dragon painted on the lid. Each piece was covered in a fine, black dust. Casey picked up a piece of red glass from the box and examined it.

"The police just brought that back," Mrs. Anderson gestured to the box as she came into the room with a tray of drinks and cookies. "They were trying to get finger prints, but all they got were mine, my daughter's, and some from a few friends. I know they would never do this."

Mrs. Anderson set the tray on top of a stack of books on the coffee table and shook her head sadly. Casey saw tears well up in the corner of her eyes, but then she looked around and smiled sadly. "I figured since the shelves were empty anyway, it's a good time to give them a good scrubbing. It's been awhile."

They spent the afternoon scrubbing shelves and refilling them with the books. Mrs. Anderson told funny stories about things that had happened in the library over the years and kept a steady stream of cookies and drinks coming from the kitchen. She let Sara help bake several batches of cookies and carry out some of the drinks. By late afternoon, she seemed to be in very good spirits.

"I still don't get it," Casey said. "Why would they trash your place like they did and not take anything? What were they looking for?"

"Oh, but they did take something. I didn't notice it at first, not until I was checking my books against my catalog." Casey looked at Jessie, and they both smiled. Only a librarian would catalog her own books.

"What did they take?" Jessie asked, biting into another cookie.

"Well, it seems like such an odd thing to take. It wasn't even worth very much and—"

"So, what was it?" Sara interrupted. Jessie gave her a warning look that she promptly ignored.

"It was a small, leather-bound journal that I found in a junk shop in Spain many years ago."

"Who wrote it?" they all asked in unison.

"It was written by a man named Trinadad Tomayo way back in 1749. He wrote it while he was in prison there." Her eyes twinkled as she leaned forward in her chair and spoke in a whisper. "It seems he was a pirate."

"A pirate!" Casey exclaimed.

"Yes, dear," she said to Casey, sitting back in her chair. "And he has ties to this very island."

"*Wow*! A real pirate! I've always heard stories of pirates on the island, but I never heard of anyone really finding any buried treasure. Does the journal have a treasure map in it? Maybe that's what the burglars were after."

"Unfortunately, this journal didn't have a map or directions or any mention of a pirate's treasure. It was more the rambling of a sick man. He died in prison, and I don't think he ever even got a trial. I only bought the book because of the mention of our little island."

"I thought pirates always made a map or wrote down where their treasure was buried."

"Perhaps he did, but not in this journal. Our burglars will be mighty disappointed if that's what they were after. He does make mention of another journal, but like I said, he was quite sick. Mostly he seemed to go on and on about crazy stuff. He tells about the horrible hurricane that sank his ship, but then he gets bizarre, writing about cannibals and crabs…just crazy rambling. I imagine he was delirious with fever."

Chapter 6

Casey and Cap sat high on a sand dune watching the late afternoon sun sink slowly into the ocean. The sky was clear, and the reflection of the sun seemed to set the waves on fire.

"We've got to get that book back, Cap," Casey said. "It could have clues to buried treasure."

"I don't know, Casey. I've heard stories of buried treasure since I was just a little crab. When I was the age my grandson is now, four of us took off and went clear to the north beach. We were convinced we could find a fortune in gold and diamonds."

"Well, did you get any treasure?"

"No, what we got was grounded for a long time, if I remember right," Cap chuckled. "My parents were pretty upset. When they knew we were all okay, they got mad, but my dad told me later that he had done the same thing when he was my age."

"Yeah, my parents would have been pretty mad at me if I had taken off treasure hunting when I was that young," Casey said, staring out to sea. After a moment of silence, he looked at Cap and continued,

"Mrs. Anderson said there was a reference in the book to another journal. If we find that book, it could lead us to the other one and then maybe—"

"Your police are on the case, Casey," Cap said. "It won't take them long to find it."

"My dad said that they were treating it as a vandalism and not a robbery. They think maybe Mrs. Anderson just misplaced the book or something, but I know she didn't."

"What makes you so sure?" Cap asked with a little laugh.

"Well, gee, Cap! She catalogs everything. She was a librarian her whole life practically, and they don't just misplace books! When we were helping her put her books back on the shelves, everything had to go in by author and in alphabetical order. No, she wouldn't just lose a book."

They began walking down the beach together. The crowds were gone, and except for a few couples holding hands and talking quietly to each other, they had the beach to themselves. "Stop by my office in the morning. I'll see if any of the crabs know anything, but don't get your hopes up. She might have been mistaken, like the police say. And, even if she's not, people and crabs have been searching for buried treasure for hundreds of years. I think this whole island has been dug up at one time or another."

✳ ✳ ✳

That night, Casey went online and Googled *Trinadad Tomayo*. He spent the entire evening trying different combinations of pirates, buried treasure, and his name, finally finding a website about pirate ships that made one small reference to Tomayo.

According to the website, Trinadad Tomayo had run the waters between the Caribbean Islands and Mexico, preying on merchant ships from both Spain and Portugal, stealing gold, silver, and precious gems. His ship had been blown off course during a hurricane and ran aground on a sandbar just north of the island, where it broke apart. No other survivors were found, and as far as anyone knew, neither had the treasure.

Casey dreamed that night about pirate ships and treasure.

Chapter 7

Casey was perched on the old, rusty, folding metal chair in Cap's office in the crab town under the beach. He was watching him shuffle papers between the ever-present heaps that always seemed to clutter Cap's desk. Cap had his reading glasses on, and clutching a pen awkwardly in his claw, he scribbled on a few papers before he pushed the glasses up to the top of his head and looked at Casey.

"I caught four of our young crabs sneaking back into the crab hole in the wee hours this morning," he said to Casey. "I don't know what these kids are thinking these days!" Leaning back in his leather upholstered chair, he smiled. "Oh, I guess I do. I was the same way, bored with the crab town and looking for adventure. Anyway, they were hanging out up at the Coconut Cabanas restaurant. They've got live music up there at night, and the young crabs like to go up there and dance on the beach. Two of them overheard a couple of men talking about the break-in so they crept up close to them."

"Holy cow, Cap! This is great! What did they say? Did they admit they did it? Do they have the book?"

"Hold on, Casey. One question at a time, okay?"

"Oh, sorry. Cap."

"First off," Cap explained, "these kids were playing around, double-daring each other to get close enough to touch their feet, so I don't think they were paying too much attention to the conversation." Cap smiled. "When I was young, I always went for the feet of ladies who were wearing little sandals. I always got a good scream out of 'em."

"Oh, rats!" Casey said dejectedly.

"It's not all bad. They heard them talk about going back to Mrs. Anderson's house. They seem to think she knows more or may even have the other journal. Plus—and this is a big plus—we know they are staying in a two-bedroom cabana right on the beach. It shouldn't be hard to figure out which one." Cap reached behind and grabbed his hat from the giant, shiny fish hook attached to the wall. Placing his glasses on the desk, he plopped the hat on to his head. "I'm thinking a little Kelp Kola might be just what we need to figure out our next move."

They sat at their favorite table in the little crab diner, not far from Cap's office, and ordered Kelp Kolas from Cap's daughter. As Delores set down two big, frosty mugs of Kelp Kola, Casey thanked her and then said to Cap, "Do you think they would have the journal with them in the room?"

"Well, yes. I don't see them carrying it around. It seems like they would want it safely out of sight. If we could figure out which cabana they're in, we could wait until they leave for dinner or something and sneak in." Cap paused and took a long swig of Kelp Kola from his mug. Wiping the foam off his mouth with his claw, he went on, "We could steal the book back, look for clues to the treasure, and return it to Mrs. Anderson before they even know it's gone."

"What if she thinks we broke into her house and stole it? She might think that I'm returning it because I feel guilty or something."

Cap thought for a while. Anyone who knew Casey would know that he didn't steal that journal and trash Mrs. Anderson's house. He was just not that kind of person. He didn't lie, he didn't steal, and he always kept his word. Still, as soon as the thugs realized that the book was gone, they would flee the island and never get caught.

"Okay, how about this. We watch the cabana until they leave. Then we search it and find where they are keeping the journal. If we can find it quick enough, we would have time to look through it for clues. Then we put it back, call the police anonymously, tell them we saw the book with the two thugs, and they take it from there."

"I don't know, Cap. It might work, though. I know the Coconut Cabanas; my parents take me there for dinner once in a while. There's only two of the two-bedroom units on the beach. The rest of them are toward the back, facing the pool. We should be able to tell right away which one the robbers are in. But, how will we get in? They'll lock the door when they leave, especially if the journal is in there."

Cap just smiled. He picked up his hat and, setting it on top of his shiny blue head, he said, "You just leave that to me, my friend."

Chapter 8

The sun was low in the sky as Casey approached the crab hole. He was just about to crawl in when he heard Cap come up behind him completely out of breath from running.

"Boy, am I glad to see you!" he wheezed. "I just left the Cabanas, and I know which one they're in!"

"Great, Cap! How did you find out?"

"Come on, I'll explain on the way." He scampered around the big sand dune toward the beach. At this hour, the crowds had thinned out, but there were still several large groups of people hanging out to see the sunset. Casey and Cap kept close to the dunes so Cap wouldn't be seen and quickly made their way down the beach.

"We have to be quick if we want time to read the journal," Cap explained as they hurried along. "I was staking out the two cabanas all afternoon. One of them is rented by a family with totally rambunctious twin boys, maybe four years old. Didn't figure they would be trashing somebody's home so I watched the other one. Sure enough, about ten minutes ago I saw two men come out. One of 'em is real tall and skinny. He wears glasses, and he had on a bowtie…looks like a real professor type. The other guy is the exact opposite. That guy must weigh four hundred pounds. A real slob, stained t-shirt and nasty looking jeans that barely cover his rump. I don't know where they were going. Neither of them said a word, so I don't know how long they'll be gone."

When they reached the Coconut Cabanas, the twin boys were in the middle of a major tantrum, throwing themselves around on the front porch that was shared by the two attached cabanas. The boy's parents pleaded and bribed as the boys squabbled and fussed, and it seemed to Casey that they would never leave. In the end it was promises of ice cream and new toys that got the boys to go along, hand-in-hand with their parents, to dinner. Even when he was only four years old, Casey knew his parents had never bribed him like that. A tantrum like that would have landed him in his room without even his old toys.

When the family finally disappeared around the corner, Casey and Cap snuck up to the front door of unit 4B. Using a plastic card and a piece of thick, copper wire, Cap had the door open in less than a minute. Casey felt a moment of guilt. This was like breaking and entering, but he knew that without the journal they couldn't call the police, and the men would get away. Plus, he really wanted to read the journal.

Once inside, they turned on their flashlights. They were in a living room with a sofa and two chairs arranged around an entertainment center with a large flat-screen TV. The furniture was all rattan, painted white, with overstuffed blue and white cushions with sailboats and anchors on them. The walls were painted a pale yellow and covered with pictures of lighthouses and sailboats.

As Cap scanned the entertainment center, Casey quickly checked under the cushions of the chairs and sofa. Finding nothing in the living room, they made their way down the hall and into the first bedroom. It was decorated similar to the living room. The spread on the queen-size bed was covered with sailboats, seagulls, and pelicans in a pale yellow and light blue. As he entered the room, Casey swung his flashlight back and forth and was startled when he saw a large pelican sitting on the rattan dresser right next to him. Backing away, he flashed the light directly on the large bird only to realize that it was a ceramic lamp shaped and painted exactly like the big brown pelicans that swooped along the shoreline. The eyes seemed to be staring right at him, and it took a moment for his heart to stop racing.

Cap went directly to the closet and opened the door. A few clothes were hanging neatly on the rod, and a pair of brown leather loafers was on the floor. This was obviously the "professor's" room. Other than those few items, the closet was empty. Casey was rummaging through the drawers in the dresser. Only two of the drawers had anything in them—some underwear and socks in one drawer and a pair of perfectly folded pajamas and a new dress shirt, still in the plastic, in the other. Casey felt very uncomfortable digging into a stranger's personal belongings. He was just about to voice his opinion when Cap spoke in a whisper.

"Nothing under the mattress, either. Let's check the other bedroom before they show up."

Moving down the narrow hallway, they passed a small bathroom. Cap shone his light into the room but did not stop, apparently thinking that would not be a good place to hide the journal. In the second bedroom, at the very end of the hall, they both stopped and stared. The room looked like someone had already broken in and ransacked the place. There were clothes all over the floor, and the lamp on the dresser, made to look like a light house, was tipped over, the lampshade lying on the floor. Beside the bed was an old pizza box with two stale pieces of greasy pizza still in it. The closet door was standing open and empty except for one old, scuffed tennis shoe.

"Wow," Casey said quietly. "My mom would kill me if my room looked like this."

All six of the drawers in the dresser were empty except for a Styrofoam clam-shell, the kind you get for take-out food or a doggie bag. The smell that came out when Casey opened the drawer was so disgusting that he slammed the drawer shut without even opening the container. He turned to see Cap pulling a chicken bone out from under the mattress. Throwing the bone on the floor, Cap muttered, "This guy's sick! He should be in jail just for being such a pig!"

"It's not here, Cap. The journal isn't here. Now what?"

"I don't know. I was sure they would leave it behind, but they must have taken it with them."

"Do you think we have the wrong guys? I mean, maybe they aren't even the ones and they were just talking, you know, like they read about it in the paper, and they were just talking..."

"Nope, my cop radar is tingling. You know what that means!"

Casey shook his head. "I don't know, Cap, we broke in, and we didn't find anything. I think..."

Chapter 9

They heard a faint click as the front door was unlocked. Until that very moment, neither of them had noticed the windows, or lack of, in this back bedroom. Because the back of the cabana faced an alley, there were clear blocks built high into the walls along two sides of the room. These allowed light to come in without subjecting the guests to a view of the alley and dumpster right behind the cabanas. Casey and Cap shut off their flashlights and, sneaking to the door, peered down the hallway.

As the front door slowly opened, they were able to see two silhouettes against the security light located just outside. As Cap had said, one was very tall and slender, and the other was huge. He seemed to block out the light in the entire doorway as he entered. Casey gasped, and Cap put his claw on his arm. He put his other claw to his lips, indicating that Casey needed to be very quiet. Standing on either side of the doorway, they continued to peer down the hallway.

"I still can't believe that we went to all that trouble, and the dang book isn't even in English," the large man growled as he headed down the hall.

"Of course it's not, you dolt!" replied the tall, thin man. "Tomayo was a Spaniard. He wrote in Spanish. It doesn't take a rocket scientist to figure that out. That's why I'm reading it, and you're not. I'll let you know what I find out."

The large man stopped halfway down the hallway and turned. "How do I know you ain't gonna lie to me?"

"You don't!" he spat back. "Unfortunately, I still need you to do the more, shall we say, *unsavory* work. You'll also be good at the digging and lifting when we find the treasure. Now, I'm going to the library before it closes. I want to follow up on the ship, the *Santa Antonita*. There might be some information there."

"Yeah, yeah, Per-fess-er," the fat man said sarcastically. "You just do that. I'm gonna take a nap."

He turned and stomped down the hall. Casey and Cap pulled back from the door and looked around frantically. At the last moment, Casey saw Cap duck into the closet as he dived under the bed.

The queen-size bed had been pushed against the wall because the room was so small. As Casey dived under it, he grabbed a corner of the white and blue quilt that was on the floor, pulling it partially under the bed with him and blocking any view of him. As he lay there listening to his heart pound, he became aware of a nasty stench, like rotten eggs mixed with the smell of the locker room at the school gym. When the big man came into the room and turned on the light, Casey could see that his nose was just inches from a scuffed and dirty tennis shoe, the match to the one in the closet. His eyes began to water, but he didn't dare move and risk making a sound.

The big man took three steps and threw himself onto the bed as he let out a huge burp. Casey rolled away from the shoe and up against the wall just as the man hit the bed. The springs groaned under the tremendous weight and began to sag until they were nearly to the floor. If Casey had been there, he would surly have been crushed! Although he felt lucky at not being crushed, he realized that he was trapped. The headboard and footboard of the bed came clear to the floor, leaving no avenue of escape there, and with the springs practically resting on the floor at the center of the bed, there was nowhere to go. He was stuck!

Casey was lying on his side, his back against the wall, with one arm over his head. There was barely enough room to breathe, and the big man rolled over, closer to the wall, squeezing him into an even tighter space. He tried to see past the springs and quilt to see if Cap was still in the closet, but there was not enough room to see anything but a thin strip of light reflected off the hardwood floor. The smell under the bed was making him nauseated, and he was beginning to think he should take his chances with the big man rather than suffocate in this tiny, stinky space when the big man rolled back over and got out of the bed.

Hoping that the man would not decide to lie back down, Casey took several deep breaths and crawled to the edge of the bed. He could see the man standing by the closet scratching his abundant belly and yawning loudly, and then he saw him start down the hallway toward the bathroom. As soon as the bathroom door closed, Casey was on his feet and running as fast as he could down the hall for the front door. He didn't even attempt to be quiet about it, he just wanted out! Cap was right behind him, his claws tap-tapping on the tile in rhythm with Casey's beating heart. Slamming the door behind them, they ran down the beach and into the darkness before the big man could follow.

Chapter 10

Casey met Cap at the library when it opened at exactly 8:00 a.m. Sitting under one of the flowering bougainvillea bushes that lined the wide sidewalk, they watched as Mr. Crandall walked up to the glass front doors and dug through his briefcase for the keys.

"Okay, I'll be at the backdoor waiting for you to let me in," Cap whispered.

"What are we looking for anyway, Cap?" Casey asked, yawning. He'd had to get up early to get his chores done before he left and wasn't sure what the hurry was.

"I'm not sure," Cap said quietly. "Whatever the 'Professor' was looking for. He said something about the *Santa Antonita* so I guess we should start there."

Casey entered the library by the front door saying a quick good morning to Mr. Crandall, who was standing behind a large circular desk in the middle of the reading room. There were several sofas and a dozen high-backed chairs located near the desk by the floor-to-ceiling windows at the front of the building.

Mr. Crandall stopped what he was doing and eyed Casey suspiciously but did not speak. He was dressed in his usual long-sleeved white shirt and gray vest with black dress slacks. Because he was so tall and gangly, his shirt sleeves and slacks always seemed a little too short, like he had outgrown them or was wearing his little brother's clothes. He always had tiny wire-rimmed glasses perched on his pointed nose that he perpetually peered over, and Casey had never seen him without his black necktie.

He made his way quickly past the desk and down one of the long aisles of books toward the back of the library. Other than Mr. Crandall, he was the only person in the library at this early hour so he tried to walk quietly and not draw attention to himself. When he reached the back wall, he made his way directly to the small back door, hoping it would open from the inside without a key and without setting off an alarm. When he reached the door, he looked back, and not seeing Mr. Crandall, he put his hand on the bar that would open the door.

Mr. Crandall seemed to appear out of nowhere and grabbed his arm. "What do you think you're doing, boy?" Casey's mind went blank; he just stared at the librarian. "Well, what do you have to say?"

"I...uh...I...thought this was the restroom, sir."

"You're in a library, and you can't read?" Mr. Crandall said sarcastically. "'Emergency Exit,'" he read, pointing to the sign on the door.

"Oh, wow. I'm sorry. I guess I have to go really bad."

The librarian looked at Casey for a long time and then turned and pointed to the far wall where the men's room was located. "Don't leave a mess in there, do you hear?"

"Yes, sir. Thank you." Casey hurried in the direction the man was pointing. He could feel the man's eyes boring into his back all the way. The door to the men's room was slightly ajar, and Casey quickly entered and closed the door behind him. Leaning against the closed door, he closed his eyes and let out a sigh of relief.

"The old bathroom story will get 'em every time."

Casey nearly jumped out of his flip-flops! "Cap, how did you get in here? I never even got close to getting that door open."

"I figured old Crandall would follow you so I just waited until he did and slipped right in through the front door.

"Great, so now what?"

"Now, you're going back to chat up Crandall out there. Ask him about pirate ships that came to the island and ask him where information on the *Santa*

Antonita would be. I'll hang back, and when you get something, meet me at the back wall."

"I don't know, Cap, he's such a grouch," Casey said, shaking his head.

"Yeah, but that's his job—to help people—so get out there, and make him work a little," Cap insisted.

As Casey approached the front desk, he noticed that several of the chairs were now occupied by older men reading newspapers or books. There were also two young women with eight two-to-four-year-olds in tow, headed for the little children's story room. Casey had spent many hours in that room when he was little. It was furnished with brightly colored beanbag chairs and tiny, kid-sized tables and chairs. There were puzzles and stuffed animals and about a zillion storybooks.

"Excuse me," he said to Mr. Crandall, "I was kind of looking for information about pirate ships on the island, you know, like back in the olden days."

"Did you even try the card catalog? That's what it's there for, you know." Mr. Crandall looked over his glasses at Casey with a look that suggested he found him to be as distasteful as a slimy bug.

"Well, um...yes, sir, but I was hoping to find out about the *Santa Antonita*, and well, I really wasn't sure...I mean, the card catalog isn't like Googling, you know...uh...sir."

"Why the sudden interest in that old ship? You're the second person to ask in two days. I'll tell you exactly what I told the other guy."

"Oh, that would be great!"

"Back in the history section, look for a book called *Pirates and Ship Wrecks* written by a fellow named Carson. As far as I know, that's the only reference in the library that mentions your ship."

"Thank you, Mr. Crandall."

"When you're done, young man, make sure you bring that book back up here to me. You kids are always putting them back on the shelf out of order."

Casey barely heard him because he was already headed down the long aisle toward the history section.

Chapter 11

They sat on the floor at the very end of the aisle with their backs against the end of the seven-foot-tall bookshelves. Casey sat cross-legged with the large book open in his lap, flipping through the pages; Cap sat next to him. There were sketches and full-page drawings of ships from the 1700s and 1800s. The author had written a short description of each of the ships along with its history and any details available on how and when they wrecked. Most of these ships had been sailing to and from Mexico with trade goods and treasure when they were blown off course and ended up far to the north on one of the many barrier islands that lined the coast here.

Some of the ships that sank in these parts were fleeing from pirates, and unable to outrun them, they were forced to stand their ground here. As they battled, one or the other of the ships, and sometimes both, would be sunk; oftentimes the treasure went down with the ship. Other times, the ships were blown off course by the violent hurricanes that could come up, many times with little or no advance warning.

As Casey flipped through the book, his mind began to wander. *How much gold and silver must still be out there, buried on the ocean floor, for hundreds of years?* He turned the page while deep in thought.

"Hey, hey, go back," Cap said.

He flipped back, and there was a full-page drawing of the pirate ship *Dragon's Fire*. Under the picture the caption read, *Captain Trinadad Tomayo, sole survivor.*

According to the legend, Tomayo and his crew were able to capture the Portuguese merchant ship, *Dragon's Fire*. They set the crew adrift in lifeboats and armed the ship with canons. With this large, well-armed ship, they were able to sail between the Caribbean Islands and Mexico, stealing treasure and sinking ships. The *Dragon's Fire* ran aground in a hurricane after being blown off course, and only Trinadad Tomayo is known to have survived.

The story said that he may have been able to save the treasure on board and hide it here on the island. No one is sure if this is true or not because no treasure has ever been found. By the time he was rescued by the Spanish galleon *Santa Antonita* he had a horrible tropical disease probably carried by the mosquitoes. Suffering from high fevers and severe thirst, he had gone insane. When asked about the treasure, he would only mumble about cannibals, crabs, and other crazy things. While in prison in Spain, he had kept a journal full of bizarre stories and crazy talk. He died in prison late in 1749.

Chapter 12

Casey kept Mr. Crandall occupied while Cap slipped out the front door, unseen. They met up at Cap's office later that day. Casey put his flip-flops on the seat of the rusty folding metal chair and sat on them, trying not to get any more rust stains on the back of his shorts.

"What a waste of time! We pretty much knew all that stuff already. What we need is that journal."

Cap leaned way back in his chair and put his claws behind his head. "I agree. We gotta see what that journal says, but what bothers me most right now is getting those two thugs behind bars. No one should get away with treating a lady that way, crab or human."

"We can't call the police until we know exactly where the journal is. That's our only evidence. If the cops get there and can't find the journal, they'll think it was just a crank call and it would tip off the thugs," Casey said.

"That's exactly what I was thinking. We know it's the professor-type that has it. He's the one we need to watch. He's not going to let it out of his sight. He needs it to find the original journal."

"Hey, how about we plant a tape recorder in their living room. Maybe he'll tell the other guy something and—"

"Nah, it didn't sound like he trusts the fat man enough to tell him anything. I know I wouldn't. He's such a big pig, he'd probably blab it all around town for a bucket of fried chicken." Cap sat straight up in his chair. "They spend a lot of time away from the cabana. I don't know where they go, but let's head back there later and sneak in. We'll hide out in the professor's room and see what he does with it before he goes out for dinner."

"Gosh, Cap. What if we get caught?"

"We won't. We'll stay hidden until they both go out, and then we'll slip out. We'll call the police with the information from the phone in the cabana, and we'll be gone before anyone can connect us."

"But then we won't get to see what's in the journal."

"Sure we will. The police will give the journal back to Mrs. Anderson, who will be happy to let you borrow it for a while. If we want to get those guys, we'll just have to be patient. After all, that treasure has been buried for over two hundred years. A few more days won't make any difference."

"I guess so," Casey said, the disappointment evident in his voice.

"Heck, maybe you should give the cops your name. You'll be a big hero again."

"Actually, we better make the call anonymous. My mom might not understand about me breaking into people's rooms at night, even if it is to catch the bad guys."

"You're probably right, but it is a shame," Cap said.

Chapter 13

The clouds obscured the moon and stars, leaving the beach in almost total darkness. Casey could just make out the white crests of the waves as they broke just off shore and rolled in one after the other. When they reached the cabanas, there was no sign of the twins or their parents, but the two robbers were there on the front porch, just leaving. The fat man was unscrewing the bulb from the security light mounted on the wall between the two cabanas.

"Hurry up, will ya?" the professor hissed. "I just want to get this over with."

Just before the light went out, Casey saw the fat man turn and smile. "What's the matter?" he heard the big man say. "The big, smart man too queasy for the job? You didn't seem to have a problem trashing the old lady's house."

"Just shut up, and let's go!"

"Sure thing," said the fat man, hitching up his jeans shorts. "Personally, I think this is the fun part of the job, ya know?"

Cap and Casey stood still in the shadows of an overgrown flowering shrub in a planter next to the twins' side of the cabanas. They watched as the men walked up toward the parking lot. Casey started toward the cabana, but Cap stopped him. "They might come back. Let's just make sure they really leave first. I don't know what they're planning to do, but I really don't like the sound of it."

They waited until the car was safely headed down the street before approaching the porch. In the darkness, Cap fumbled and dropped the wire he was using to pop the lock. Casey got on his hands and knees, feeling around in the dark for the thick piece of copper. When his hand finally found it, he had been brushing back and forth with his hand, and he had pushed the wire right to the edge of the board. Picking it up, he gave a sigh of relief that he had not pushed it any further or it would have gone between the boards and down under the little porch into the sand.

"Why would he unscrew the light bulb?" Casey asked.

"Obviously they don't want anyone to see them when they come back. Or maybe they don't want anyone to see what they are bringing back." Cap made quick work of the lock and soon he and Casey were standing in the living room for the second time.

"We can be pretty sure the journal isn't in the fat man's room, and it probably isn't in this room, but we should give it a quick check anyway," Cap said to Casey.

"Thank goodness we don't have to go back in the fat man's room. That place just stinks," Casey said, wrinkling his nose.

Turning on his flashlight, Casey began looking under the sofa and chair cushions again while Cap checked the cabinets in the entertainment center. A quick check of the tiny kitchen turned up nothing. Casey checked the refrigerator and found half of an old pizza, some boxes of Chinese take-out that were turning green, and three cans of beer. The cabinets were completely bare, and the trash can under the sink was overflowing with fast food wrappers and containers and empty beer cans. "You'd think that fat slob could at least recycle the cans," Casey muttered to himself.

They had obviously opted not to pay for daily maid service, probably for privacy. Cap checked the small bathroom and came up empty handed, as well.

In the professor's room, they found the bed neatly made. In the closet, two pairs of shoes were set side-by-side on the floor, and several pair of slacks and three white shirts were hung evenly spaced across the bar above them—the shirts on the right and the slacks on the left. Tucked into the corner of the closet was a small black suitcase. Upon inspection, they found the suitcase was empty.

When he opened the top-right-hand drawer of the six-drawer dresser, Cap found stacks of neatly folded undershirts, some socks, and underwear folded into neat little squares.

"Man, this guy is a total neat-freak. He's as neat as fat guy is filthy," Cap whispered. "Makes me wonder how two so totally opposite people work together in a life of crime. I'm surprised they ever met."

Casey was lying on the floor, shining his light back and forth under the bed. "Yeah, in a way, this is just as creepy as the other room. I mean, it just isn't normal."

The rest of the drawers were empty with the exception of one neatly folded pair of pajamas. There was nothing under the bed so they thought that the professor probably had the journal with him.

"It just doesn't seem right to me," Cap said as he ran his claw between the mattress and box springs. "He's a smart guy, this professor, and I can't see him risking getting caught carrying that journal around. We're missing something, Casey. I just don't know what."

Casey sat on the floor, trying to think where the journal could be hidden. Mrs. Anderson had said that it was a small book, about the size of a diary, bound in leather and tied with string because the binding had cracked over time.

"Maybe it's in their car."

"Maybe. Tell me again what you found in the kitchen, and don't leave anything out." Cap sat on the chair next to the bed and closed his eyes. He listened intently as Casey went through everything he had seen in the kitchen.

"...and the trash was overflowing. There was nothing in the drawers except stuff that's supposed to be there, you know, silverware, spatulas, a lime-squeezer, oh, and one drawer had a roll of silver duct tape. And the refrigerator was—"

"Hold it! That's it!"

"What's it?"

"The duct tape. Of course, how stupid can I be? I can't believe I didn't think of it sooner!" Cap banged the side of his head with his claw and jumped off the chair. Crawling under the bed, he began to shine the light straight up, looking between the springs. Casey crawled under the bed next to Cap and asked, "What, Cap, what did we miss?"

Crawling out from under the bed, Cap hurried to the dresser and pulled the empty drawers completely out of it. He checked the bottom of each drawer and began shining the light to the back and top of each opening.

"He would have taped it up someplace that no one would think to look." The last drawer that he pulled out was the one the professor was using for his socks and underwear. Careful not to mess up the neat little stacks of clothes, Cap put the drawer on the floor and peered inside. He reached in, and Casey could hear the sound of duct tape being ripped off wood.

"We've got it!" Cap said triumphantly!

"Cap, you're a genius! Let me see it!" Casey said excitedly.

Cap was just about to let Casey take the little book from him when he pulled back. "No, wait. We can't have your fingerprints on it. If they find your prints on the book, those crooks will say you planted it, and it will be your word against theirs."

Pulling his hand back, Casey said, "You're right, as usual. So, go ahead, open it. You're the one who's fluent in Spanish anyway. Come on, come on! What does it say?"

Chapter 14

Cap sat down on the floor next to the drawer of underwear and began quietly reading and translating. It was slow-going at first because many of the words spoken in Spain in the 1740s were different from the Spanish spoken in Mexico and the United States today. Also, as Mrs. Anderson had said, Trinadad Tomayo did seem insane. At times, his writing was lucid, and at other times, he just seemed to rant incoherently. He wrote at length about his life as a pirate, and expressed great regret over the loss of his crew.

Sitting in the quiet, dark room, reading by the light of the flashlight, they lost track of time. Cap was reading about the storm that had blown them off course and led to the sinking of the *Dragon's Fire* when they heard the men outside, struggling up the three steps to the porch. Quickly, Cap replaced the book at the back of the opening, rubbing back and forth across the tape to be sure that it stuck good. He had just gotten the drawer pushed back into the dresser when the front door opened.

He motioned for Casey to get under the bed and then followed him. As they lay on the floor, they could hear grunting from the big man and then a thump, as if something heavy was dropped on the floor.

"You idiot! There is no need for that!" Softening his voice, the professor said, "Let me help you, ma'am. I apologize for the clumsiness of my *friend* here." The word friend dripped with sarcasm. "Let me help you to a chair."

From their hiding place under the bed, they could hear scuffling and then a woman's scream was cut off before it could be heard outside the walls of the cabana. Casey's heart began to beat wildly.

"My dear lady," the professor said, "I am so sorry, but you were warned to keep quiet. Please do understand that I really do not wish to harm you in any way. My little friend, on the other hand, well, sometimes I just cannot seem to control him."

As silently as possible, Casey and Cap crept down the hall. As he moved slowly, Casey was convinced that the two men would hear his heart pounding. They were peeking around the corner into the living room. What Casey saw both angered and frightened him. The large man had hold of both of Mrs. Anderson's arms, and he was wrestling her into one of the chairs. The professor had the roll of duct tape and was tearing off a long piece. A shorter piece of the tape had already been secured across Mrs. Anderson's mouth, and as she was forced into the chair, he began wrapping the long piece of tape around her arm and the arm of the chair. He secured her other arm in the same fashion.

With Mrs. Anderson's arms secure, the tall man ripped off another long piece of tape and bent to wrap it around her leg and the leg of the chair. The instant he touched her leg, she began to kick wildly, landing several hard blows first on the professor's head and then on his chest. The big man stepped back, making no attempt to help his partner and began to laugh.

"What's so funny, you big oaf? Get over here, and help me with her."

"Gee, you were doing so well without my help." The big man laughed. Reaching down, he grabbed both of Mrs. Anderson's ankles and slammed them harshly against the legs of the chair. The professor quickly taped her ankles in place.

Casey knew they were in trouble! He was so angered by what he saw that he stood and was just about to go into the living room to demand that they release the old librarian, but his knees began to tremble, and he kneeled back down in the hallway. Cap pulled him back and motioned toward the bedroom.

"I know you want to help her, but you're not going to be much help to her taped up to the other chair," Cap whispered when they were safely back in the bedroom. "We gotta use our brains. We have a few things going for us, like the fact that they don't know we're here. That's our one big advantage right now, so don't go barging out there like the cavalry and lose that for us."

Casey took a deep breath and then another. Cap was right. There wasn't much a little boy and a crab could do in a physical fight with two grown men, three if you counted the fat man as two, and he was plenty big enough to be two men.

"Okay, what do we do now? What's the plan?" he asked.

"I don't know. I don't have one." Casey turned and started for the door, but Cap grabbed his arm and continued. "*Yet*. We need to know what their plan is. So far, she's okay. Looks more mad than afraid, so that's good. Now, come on, and *be quiet*!"

The two of them crept back down the hall and peeked around the corner again. Mrs. Anderson's eyes were blazing. Casey had always known her as a sweet and gentle person. He had never seen her angry before, but it was obvious that she was furious.

"...as long as you don't scream. Is that understood?" The professor reached over and ripped the duct tape from her mouth. She instantly began to scream, and the tape was immediately put back over her mouth.

"It's just a few questions, nothing too terribly hard, and then you're free to go. I suppose if you really want to do this the hard way..." Looking at the fat man, the professor shrugged and said, "You still fighting that urge of yours?"

The big man smiled broadly, showing tobacco-stained teeth. He reached into his pocket and pulled out a cigarette lighter. Putting the lighter right in front of Mrs. Anderson's face, he flicked it on, moving the flame back and forth in front of her a few times.

"I'm afraid that my little friend is a bit of a pyromaniac. He likes to burn things down," the professor said in an almost friendly tone. "And while I try my best to help him control his urges, well, you know. Your pretty little house has been on his mind since we got to the island. I, personally, would hate to see it burned to the ground." Casey watched the fiery anger in Mrs. Anderson's eyes disappear and be replaced with fear. She began to cry quietly. "So, do you think you could answer a few simple questions now?"

Slumping in her chair, Mrs. Anderson nodded her head yes.

Quietly, Cap and Casey started back down the hall toward the bedroom only to become aware that the professor was headed their way. They ducked into the bedroom and dived under the bed just as the light was turned on. Casey lay still on his stomach trying to control his breathing and still his beating heart.

The tall man gently removed the drawer with the neat stacks of underwear and placed it on top of the dresser. Reaching to the back of the opening, he pulled out the little journal and set it next to the drawer. They watched from their hiding place as he carefully replaced the drawer, straightening each little stack before closing the drawer.

The professor took a step back and began to flip through the little book. Trying to get a better look at what the man was doing, Casey used his toes to push himself closer to the edge of the bed. To his horror he saw his pack still sitting on the chair where he had left it! If the man turned around, he would see it immediately!

Casey began to feel panic creep in! He reached for the pack, but it was out of reach, and they were trapped! He had visions of the big man burning his house down, and everything began to close in. It was stuffy and hot under the bed, and he found himself gasping for breath!

Cap put his big claw on Casey's arm reassuringly and winked at him. The professor, having found what he was looking for, turned off the light and left the room without ever turning around. Casey let out a loud sigh of relief.

Crawling out from under the bed, Cap shook his head and said, " Casey, you've got to calm down, or we're not gonna get out of here."

Casey took two very deep breaths. "I know, Cap, but—"

"Ssh, come on. Let's see what he wants."

When they reached the end of the hall, the fat man was lounging in the other chair, eating from a bag of BBQ potato chips. His hands were greasy and red, and he continually wiped them on the arm of the chair. The tall man began waving the book in front of Mrs. Anderson's face, screaming questions at her. "Where's the missing page? I know you have it so you might as well tell me now, and get it over with."

"Young man," Mrs. Anderson said angrily, "I am a librarian! I have never torn a page out of a book, *never*! How dare you accuse me—"

"Can it, lady! I want that page, and I want to know what this means!" Flipping to the back of the journal, he shoved a page close to her face.

"The man was sick!" Mrs. Anderson exclaimed angrily. "He obviously didn't know what he was saying, and even if he did, what makes you think I would know what it means?"

Cap leaned very close to Casey's ear and whispered, "It's time to call the cops." The police! Casey hadn't even thought of that! He nodded and headed back to the bedroom.

Unfortunately, the only telephone in the cabana was sitting on the little side table next to the chair currently occupied by Mrs. Anderson. The two of them pushed and tugged at the little window next to the bed, but it had been painted shut. Short of breaking the glass, it provided no way out. If he had to, Casey figured he would break the window, but he knew that the noise would bring the thugs running before they could get away. He should have borrowed his mother's cell phone. As he mentally beat himself up over it, he became aware that Cap was speaking to him.

"So, what do you think?"

"Think? I'm sorry, Cap, tell me again. I was kind of not listening."

"Casey, you gotta concentrate, okay? Now, listen up. The breaker box is in the back room, the fat man's room. If one of us throws the main breaker, maybe both of them will come running to check why the electricity is out. Then one of us can get into the living room, grab the cordless handset from its cradle, and then we meet back here under the bed. When they get the lights back on and start in on Mrs. Anderson again, we dial 911 and wait for the action to begin."

Casey didn't really want to leave the safety of the little room. He wanted to crawl back under the bed and stay there until the police came. "Okay, that's a good plan," he said. "Who should do what?"

"I don't know, but maybe you should get the phone. Poor Mrs. Anderson has been through enough without bumping into big, beautiful me," Cap said, smiling.

Despite his fear and anger, Casey couldn't help but smile. "All right, I'll meet you back here, and then we'll make the call."

Chapter 15

Lying on the hardwood floor under the bed, Casey could hear the faint tapping of Cap's claws as he made his way to the rear bedroom. He had inched up to the very edge of the bed in order to get out quickly when he heard the men go by. This would only work if both men went to check out the source of the power failure. As he lay there, Casey could feel the tension building. Just as he began to wonder what was taking so long, the lights went out, plunging the entire cabana into darkness.

Springing from under the bed, he could hear the startled voices of the two men in the living room as he sprinted to the bedroom door. His plan was to hide behind the door as the men went by, but having misjudged the door's position, he ran headlong into the edge of it, only avoiding falling on his rump by grabbing onto the door handles on either side. He could hear the professor yelling for a flashlight as he slid behind the door, silently rubbing the bump on his head. It took only a minute, and the two men were thundering down the hall behind a weak, yellow light from a flashlight with very little battery left.

Feeling his way through the darkness and relying on his memory of the room in front of him, Casey quickly made his way to the telephone. Shoving the phone into the oversized pocket of his shorts, he turned to make his way back to the bedroom before the lights came on again. His eyes had finally adjusted to the darkness, and as he turned to leave, he caught sight of Mrs. Anderson staring at him.

Although he could not see her face clearly, he felt certain that she must be afraid. Putting his hand over hers, he leaned in and whispered, "It's okay. We're calling the cops now." Casey dived under the bed just as the lights came back on.

He could feel the phone pressing against his hip as he waited for Cap to return. Several times he reached for the phone to dial 911 but stopped himself. For some reason, he wanted Cap there when he did. It felt like an hour before he saw Cap come around the corner and slide under the bed next to him. Pulling the phone out of his pocket, he smiled at Cap and dialed the emergency number, silently practicing what he would say.

In the living room he heard a shout. The professor was screaming about the phone! How did he know? But Casey already knew. The light on the phone cradle must have come on when Casey activated the phone, and since it was right there next to Mrs. Anderson, it would be pretty hard to miss.

"Someone's in here! Search the place, and find him!"

Casey held his breath waiting for the phone to ring on the other end. He counted the seconds as they passed. One, one thousand. Two, one thousand. When he reached five, he heard the first ring and the thunder of footsteps in the hall at the same time.

With no time to think, he handed the telephone to Cap and said, "Don't let them find this!" Before Cap could respond, Casey was out from under the bed and gone. Running into the hallway, he turned toward the living room as fast as he could, running right into the big man. He bounced off the man's enormous belly and landed on his back with a loud *oomph*.

Chapter 16

"911. What is the nature of your emergency? Hello? This is 911, what is your emergency? Chris, I'm not getting anything, but the line is still open."

"You better trace the call. It could be a heart attack or something. Get some units over there right away, and keep trying."

The telephone was wedged between the bedsprings in the far corner by the wall and the headboard, well out of reach. The voices were audible only if you were lying on the floor next to the bed. Cap was behind the shower curtain in the bathroom, planning a diversion, if necessary, to get Casey out.

Meanwhile, Casey had been thrown onto the sofa, and the two men were leaning over him, the professor screaming in his face. "Who'd you call? Where is the phone? So help me, this is not a game! Tell me!"

The big man stood close, smiling in silence and pounding one oversized fist into his other hand. To

Casey, that was scarier than all the shouting and threatening the tall, skinny man was doing.

"What are you doing here? Who did you call? Answer me!" The questions kept coming, and the tall man was getting more and more agitated. Casey's mind went blank. He knew he could count on Cap, he just couldn't think of what Cap could do to help him right now. He hoped that the 911 call had gone through. They would send the police to see why no one was there. Grabbing Casey by the front of his shirt, the professor lifted him off the sofa and brought Casey's face up to his. "Answer me!" the man screamed.

Casey fumbled for an answer as he strained to hear the sound of sirens that wasn't there. "I...I... uh..."

"Answer me, now!"

"I...was...looking for a bathroom." Even as he said it, Casey realized how lame that sounded. *The bathroom? What kind of a story was that? Who would believe that he just happened to break in and stole a phone while he was looking for a bathroom?* Well, it had worked at the library, hadn't it?

Throwing Casey back on to the sofa, the tall man's hand came up to slap Casey in the face. Casey cringed, pushing himself deep into the cushions behind him. The man stopped, his hand still in the air, at the sound of rushing water. In the bathroom the bathtub, sink, and toilet were simultaneously overflowing.

Casey wiggled out of the man's grasp, leaped over the back of the sofa, and crawled under the table, which still held the lit telephone cradle. The professor ran around the sofa and was screaming at him as he grabbed under the table for Casey's leg. Casey sprang from under the table and headed for the front door. A large hand caught him by the back of his shirt and lifted him high into the air.

Casey kicked wildly, but the big man held him out away from his body and simply laughed. Throwing Casey into the chair with the red BBQ-stained fingers, he leaned in very close. Casey could smell his sour breath, and he couldn't take his eyes off of the man's yellow teeth.

"You messed things up for us." The big man sneered. "Now I'm gonna make you pay."

He laughed and reached into his pocket. Pulling out his lighter, he clicked it on and held the flame very close to Casey's face.

A small tidal wave of water rushed down the hallway and slammed into the front door. In the distance, Casey finally heard sirens headed his way.

"The journal! Where's the journal?" the professor began screaming as he frantically searched the room.

"Hey! I'm outta here," the fat man said, heading for the front door. "That journal is nothing but a joke, and so is this whole stupid plan of yours!"

"Help me find the journal, you fool!"

The big man stepped on the empty potato chip bag that was floating on top of the pooling water in the living room. The empty bag slid across the wet tile like an ice skater on smooth ice, taking the man with it. The big man fell forward, slip-sliding on his belly right into the front door, knocking himself unconscious. Casey couldn't help but think of a beached whale as he lay there blocking the door, with water backing up behind him. A small lake was being created in the living room.

The professor, having found the journal, began pulling on one of the big man's legs trying to get him out of the way so he could open the door, but his efforts were useless. The man was just too big to budge. He ran through the little cabana, desperately searching for another way out only to realize that he was trapped. As the police cars pulled up outside, sirens blaring, he tried one last time to move the unconscious mountain of a man blocking the door. Finally, he just sat down and waited for the police.

By the time the police got the door open, using every available man to push, Casey had gently removed the tape and freed Mrs. Anderson. Before she was taken by ambulance to the hospital, she asked for a moment to speak with Casey quietly.

"Is someone else here with you, dear?"

"Uh…uh…no. Why would you ask?"

"I could have sworn you said 'we'. As in, 'We are calling the police now.'"

"Oh, I think you just misunderstood. It was just me."

"I suppose I could have been confused. Things happened so quickly, but still…oh, Casey, I am so grateful and will always be in your debt. You are truly my hero."

Casey blushed and was saved from answering when the ambulance attendants came through the door. After an hour of questions, in which Casey told the police everything he knew, or at least most of it, Officer Drew drove him home.

"That was pretty quick thinking on your part, Casey! That was quite a diversion," Officer Drew said with a chuckle. "That fat man is gonna have a really bad headache for a long time. What even made you think of overflowing the bathroom?"

"I can honestly say," Casey said with a smile, "that I don't know. It just came out of the blue."

Chapter 17

The next day, Casey met Cap at the little diner under the sand. Cap had the latest edition of the island newspaper, *The Gullwing Express*, laid out in front of him. The entire front page was dominated by the story of the arrest of the two men. Casey was hailed as a hero, though his 'uncle,' Officer Drew, had lectured him last night, telling Casey he should have called the police and not put himself in danger.

The professor and the fat man were in jail after pleading guilty to numerous charges including kidnapping and robbery. They would not be out treasure hunting anytime soon. Once he came to, the big man had told the police everything, including the fact that the tall man was indeed a professor of history and that the fat man was his brother-in-law.

As they recalled the events of last night, Cap began to laugh. "Really? Looking for the bathroom? That was the best thing you could come up with? Just how many times do you think you can use that old line?"

"Hey, Mrs. Anderson thinks I'm a hero!" Casey countered. "Besides, all you did was overflow the toilet. That's hardly what I would call a great 'cavalry to the rescue' kind of move."

Sitting in Delores's Diner with big mugs of cold Kelp Kola, the two friends laughed a long time.

"So, did you bring it?" Cap finally asked.

Reaching into his backpack, Casey pulled out the small, leather-bound journal. "I sure did!" A very grateful Mrs. Anderson had told him to keep the journal as long as he needed and any other books she had, too. She had confided to him that she thought it had all been very exciting, in a spy novel sort of way, but she was happy to have her old, non-adventurous life back.

They spent the next two hours drinking Kelp Kola, eating Delores's great cookies, and reading the journal. Cap's Spanish was flawless, and after he got used to the differences in some of the words, he was able to translate the little book with only minor difficulty. In the end, however, there was very little new information. Mrs. Anderson had been right when she said it was the ramblings of a sick man, right up to the final sentence, that is. That final sentence of the journal is what the professor had demanded that Mrs. Anderson explain. The final sentence of the journal contained only nine words: *The secret lies in the claw of the crab.*

"Whoa!" Casey whispered in awe as Cap slowly raised his big blue claw into the air. They both stared in silence as Cap turned his claw slowly, first one way and then the other.

After a very long time, in which they both closely inspected his claw, Cap picked up his Kelp Kola and said, "Rubbish!"

"You don't believe it?"

"Believe what? It doesn't mean anything. I don't know about you, but I sure don't see any secrets in this old claw."

Casey had to admit that Cap was right. They finished their Kelp Kolas and said goodbye. Casey headed out across the crabs' beautiful park toward the tunnel that lead to the beach. As he entered the tunnel, however, he stopped. Of course! It was right there in front of them all along.

He was bent over, holding his side, and out of breath as he burst into Cap's office a few minutes later.

"How could we be so stupid? It was right there, and we missed it! *We* missed it, and it should have been obvious, especially to *us*!"

"What are you talking about?" Cap asked, bewildered.

Still holding his side, he pulled the metal chair right up to Cap's desk and plopped down, not even caring about the rust stains it would leave on his shorts.

"'The secret lies in the claw of the crab,' not *your* claw. Remember, this was written over two hundred and fifty years ago."

"Okay, so what's your point?" Cap asked.

In a rush of words, Casey began to explain. "The stories all say that he was hallucinating from fever or hunger or both and that he sat on the sand dunes talking to the crabs, right? Cap, he wasn't talking to the crabs, he was talking to *one crab*, like I'm talking to you now. Two-hundred-plus years ago, a crab—maybe one of your ancestors—helped him, maybe kept him alive. Don't you see? They became friends, and they talked, like us! Anyone who might have seen it would naturally think that Trinadad was crazy, and if he tried to tell anyone the truth, they would be certain that he was crazy!"

"And he gave his secret to that crab! Casey, you're a genius," Cap said.

"Yeah, but now what?" Casey suddenly sounded dejected. "We still don't know the secret or where it is."

Cap thought about it for several minutes before he spoke. "We've been looking for secrets in the human history books. We crabs have history books, too, and our own secrets. I think that's where we should be looking."

Chapter 18

Casey couldn't help but notice that the library that served the crab colony was the exact opposite of the one he was used to. His library was a tall white building with light from floor-to-ceiling windows that made up the entire front of the building. The aisles were brightly lit by fluorescent lights and evenly spaced sky lights, and the shelves that held the books were large and white. By contrast, he and Cap had to stop just inside the door and let their eyes adjust to the dim light. Standing in the entry, Casey became aware of the fact that everything here, right down to the wooden floor, must have been salvaged over many, many years from old ship wrecks. The tall wooden shelves appeared to be made from hard, dark wood, like teak and mahogany, and, like the floor, had been polished over the years to a rich, chocolate sheen. Next to the small desk occupied by the librarian was a large ship's wheel inlaid with brass that gleamed like gold. The room smelled of wood and polish, and he noted that there was not a speck of dust anywhere.

Casey was still standing in the entry, taking it all in, when the librarian approached.

"Jethro!" she exclaimed to Cap. "It's been a long time. My goodness, I was beginning to wonder if you thought you were too smart for our old books." Turning to Casey she said, "And you must be Casey. I've heard so much about you, young man. Welcome. I must say that I believe you are the very first human to ever visit our little library." Mrs. Clemons giggled like a young girl. "It's so very exciting."

Cap cleared his throat. "Mrs. Clemons, this is Casey. Casey, Mrs. Clemons, our librarian."

Casey put his hand out and gently grasped her claw. "I'm very happy to meet you."

She was a tiny crab, especially compared to Cap, and Casey wondered just how old she was. Her delicate claws were pure white, and her shell was faded to just the slightest hint of blue. She wore tiny, wire-rimmed glasses and walked slowly but not at all stooped. There was a grace and strength about her that Casey admired.

Clearing his throat again, Cap said, "Well, Mrs. Clemons, we're kind of working on a case here and thought maybe you could help."

"Of course, Jethro. Anything I can do to help. Come, sit and tell me what you're looking for."

They sat on large, high-backed chairs with worn red cushions next to Mrs. Clemons desk and without giving too much away, told her what they had learned and what they suspected. When they were finished with their story, the old librarian leaned forward on her desk and eyed them seriously.

"Ah, a treasure hunt!" She looked at Casey for a long time without saying a word. Casey began to fidget in his seat. "And so now, here you are," she said directly to Casey, "asking about Trinadad Tomayo's secret."

"Well…uh…I guess so, uh…ma'am." They had not mentioned Tomayo by name. How did Mrs. Clemons know?

The old librarian broke into a huge smile and clapped her claws together. Her eyes danced with delight behind the lenses of her little glasses. "I always hoped it would be me, but after all these years, I had quite given up! And now, here you are! This is an exciting day, indeed." Jumping out of her chair, she started down one of the long aisles. "Come along, then, come along."

Cap and Casey sat looking at each other in confusion for a moment, and then Cap shrugged and stood up. Motioning with his claw in the direction Mrs. Clemons had gone, he said, "The lady awaits."

Casey stood and looked at Cap. "Jethro?" he asked.

Cap grunted. "Nobody calls me that anymore. And don't you—ever!"

It seemed the aisles were never ending. As one would end, it would split off into three more, each going in a different direction. By the time they approached a small door somewhere in the far reaches of the library, Casey was convinced that if anything happened to Mrs. Clemons right now, they would never find their way out. Using an old skeleton key, the librarian opened the door and entered.

They found themselves in a tiny, windowless room—more a large closet than a room, really. One bare bulb hung from the ceiling for light. Mrs. Clemons pulled the cord, but the dull, yellowish light was not enough to chase the shadows from the corners of the little room. In the middle of the room, Casey saw a small, glass-enclosed case with several books and artifacts inside. In this room the dust had not been touched, and everything was covered, as if by a thick fog. Spider webs seemed to grow out of every corner and surface, and they, too, were thick with dust. Casey leaned forward and wiped the dust off the top of the glass case to get a better look at a large, jewel-encrusted saber. One wall was lined with bookshelves crammed with old leather-bound books, their spines cracking with age.

Moving to the glass case, Mrs. Clemons slid the back open and reached inside. Using only the tip of her tiny, white claw, she pulled out a small book, bound in red leather, that had turned a deep maroon color over the years.

"When I was a young, new librarian, the responsibility of this book was passed to me. It all seemed like such an exciting adventure to me at the time, and I just couldn't wait for you to show up," she said, looking directly at Casey. "I have to admit that, as time went on, I began to doubt the stories. Certainly, at this point in my life I never thought you would show up, and I was preparing to pass this mission on to the next librarian."

"What stories? What mission?" Casey asked confused. "I don't know what you're talking about."

Setting the book on top of the glass, the old crab tapped it gently with her claw. "Hundreds of years ago, an old crab named Sculley found a half-drowned man washed ashore after a hurricane. Within a few days, the man was near death from dehydration and hunger, and old Sculley took pity on him. He brought the man water in his claw and gathered edible fish and plants, showing him what he could eat to stay alive. Over the next week, they became good friends. To show his gratitude, this man, Trinadad Tomayo, offered Sculley the only thing he had. A fortune in gold, silver, and gems that he had buried in the sand.

"But Sculley wasn't interested in treasure," Mrs. Clemons continued. "What does a crab do with gold coins anyway? No, Sculley was more interested in his friendship. During long talks on the beach while he waited for rescue, Trinadad expressed such remorse about his life, and especially about the loss of his crew. Just before he was rescued, Trinadad gave Sculley this book and asked that he keep it safe. It was to be given to any member of his crew, or their ancestors, who asked for it. Sculley gave him his solemn promise, and so, all these years later, the secret is still guarded and waiting."

"You, Casey, are the first. You are the first human to have asked, and so the journal and all the secrets it contains are now yours."

Casey's hand shook as he reached for the journal.

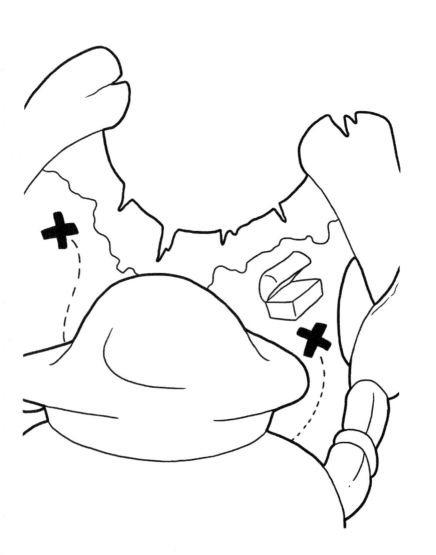

Chapter 19

They spent the rest of the afternoon in Cap's office with the door closed, reading, translating, and rereading the journal. Carefully turning each brittle page, Cap read and translated while Casey took notes. It provided a very fascinating look into the life of a pirate in the 1700s, but as Cap read on, it became more and more disturbing. Tomayo wrote of waiting in hidden coves to attack unsuspecting merchant ships and then robbing them of all of their money, jewels and goods. He named the ships that they attacked, described in detail how they captured them and seized the loot. He had even kept a fairly accurate list of the goods and money taken with each raid.

"Cap," Casey quietly interrupted.

Cap looked up from the journal. "What's wrong, Casey?"

"The buried treasure…"

"What about it?"

"The treasure…" Casey sounded a little rattled. "Well, it was all stolen. I mean…"

Cap waited for Casey to continue. When he remained silent Cap asked, "Casey, where did you think pirates got their treasures?"

"I don't know. I guess I never really thought about it. I mean, I just thought it belonged to them and they were just…I don't know. But it didn't belong to them, they were just like the professor and that fat man, just thieves!"

"Do you want me to quit reading?"

"No," Casey said. "Finish the journal."

Cap began translating again. There were not many pages left and Casey remained silent. Finally, Cap turned the page and stared at it for a long time. Slowly, he turned the little journal around so that Casey could see it. Across the final two pages was a crudely drawn map. But even after over two hundred and fifty years it was obvious that this was their island. Neither of them spoke for a long time.

"So, now what?" Cap finally asked. Casey only stared at the map looking conflicted for a while. Cap waited in silence.

Slowly, a grin began to spread across his face. "Now we go treasure hunting!"

"We do?" Cap asked.

"We do! But we don't keep the treasure!"

"We don't?"

"We don't! It didn't belong to Tomayo. He stole it, so it can't belong to us either."

"Then what do you plan to do with it, Casey?" Cap asked

"We are going to give it back!"

Cap's eyes widened in surprise and he shook his head. "Give it back to who? Casey, those people have been gone for over two hundred years."

"When we find the treasure," Casey said enthusiastically, "We give it back to the ancestors of those people."

"And just how do you propose to find those ancestors?"

Casey held up the journal. "Right here, Cap. Tomayo wrote the names of the ships he robbed. All those ships were registered, just like they are today, so there would be names of people who owned and worked on the ships. We can give it back to their families!"

"Sounds good to me," Cap said. "I wouldn't really know what to do with treasure. But do you think I could just keep…"

"Cap! We can't keep any of the treasure! That would make us just as greedy as Tomayo and the professor!"

"No, Casey, I told you I don't want any of the treasure. I just want to keep the lock from the chest. I think it would look great hanging on my wall right about there." Cap pointed to the wall above where Casey was sitting. "Just the lock."

That night, Casey had found it impossible to sleep due to the anticipation and excitement. Now, just as the sun was coming up, he waited impatiently for Cap to show up here, at the northern most tip of the island. He was aware that over two hundred years of hurricanes had changed the island, sands had shifted one way and then another, and some landmarks identified in the journal no longer existed. Still, if they carefully counted each step, he was convinced that the treasure would be found.

When Cap finally showed up, the two of them set out. Armed with a compass, a folding camp shovel, a rope, a can of orange spray paint, a camera to document the find, and a backpack full of sandwiches and water, they began counting paces. To avoid confusion and double check the count, each of them counted silently to one hundred. At one hundred paces they stopped and, using the spray paint, made a small mark in the sand. By doing this, should they lose count, they could go back to the last mark and not have to start all over again.

Following the directions, they made their way south down the beach, west into the sand dunes, south again, and back to the beach. By noon they had crisscrossed back and forth across the island between the beach and the dunes. They followed the directions exactly, heading south, then west, then north again, always counting their paces. They left a small orange mark each time they reached one hundred or changed directions. When they left a mark right next to a fallen palm tree, they stopped for lunch. They ate quickly and didn't really speak much, each of them lost in their own thoughts of pirates and treasure.

As the day wore on, they continued to cross the dunes several times. The afternoon sun seemed to scorch them, and Casey wished for at least the twentieth time that he had brought more water. His clothes and shoes were covered with grass burrs and dirt, and the little shovel seemed to weigh fifty pounds. But none of that mattered. When they reached the top of the large dune they were climbing, they would be a mere two hundred and eighty paces from the treasure!

When they reached the top of the dune, Casey stopped and stared, more than a little confused. With all the twists and turns and counting, he had paid little attention to where they were, and now, stretched out before him was the town's downtown section, with all its roads and shops and restaurants. He could see his school in the distance and along the main street, the post office and theater.

Cap sprayed a small mark next to Casey's shoe. "That's one hundred," he said. Looking past Casey, he could see the town stretched out in front of them, and his heart sank. After a moment, though, he prodded Casey on. "We're almost there. Don't give up now."

Casey took one pace and then another and quietly counted down the final paces. Down the backside of the dune, across the street, the supermarket parking lot, he continued to count, always watching the compass and staying on course. It was busy— people walking around, shopping, riding bikes— making it more difficult to concentrate. They could no longer mark every one hundred paces, Cap tried to keep to the shadows and shrubs so he wasn't seen but finally had to stop and wait for Casey to finish the hunt. It would not be good for him to be seen walking down one of the town's main streets in broad daylight.

Taking long, measured strides, he made his way to the corner, 210, across the lawn at the post office, 245, and up the wide sidewalk. He opened the glass door in front of him and continued, 273.

Two hundred seventy-eight, two hundred seventy-nine, two hundred eighty! Casey stood transfixed by the sight directly in front of him. At that very moment, a small cloud moved from in front of the sun, and Casey found himself bathed in bright light and staring at the big X right in front of him.

Well, it was sort of an X. Right there in front of him, two life-sized dolphins leaped out of the water from opposite directions, crossing each other and forming a big, blue X in the marble floor at his feet. The tiles that made up the dolphins were so perfectly inlaid in the marble floor that they looked real, and for a moment, Casey could almost feel the spray of water off their tails. Looking up, he felt the warmth of the sun shining in through the skylight two stories above him.

"What do you think you're doing in here like that?"

Casey turned to see Mr. Crandall standing behind his circular desk and staring down, over his glasses, at him. It took a moment for him to realize that he had been spoken to and that Mr. Crandall expected an answer, but he had no idea what the librarian had asked him so he kept quiet.

"Young man, this is a respectable library, not a jungle for your Indiana Jones games, as you seem to think. I will not have my library treated this way. Please take your shovel and your dirt outside, sir!"

Taking one more long look at the crossed dolphins, Casey sighed and turned to leave, dragging the shovel across the floor. "Yes, sir."

Chapter 20

Casey tentatively entered the dark crab library and stopped to let his eyes adjust to the dim light. He had just left Cap in his office, and although they had discussed it, he wasn't sure what he was going to say exactly. He almost turned to leave but stopped when he saw Mrs. Clemons slowly making her way over to him.

"Why, Casey, what a pleasant surprise." Seeing the look on his face, she reached out and took his hand in her claw. "Is everything all right, dear?"

Reaching into his pocket, he pulled out the journal and placed it gently in her claw.

"Mrs. Clemons, this doesn't belong to me. It doesn't belong to anyone really. But...well...the crabs have taken such good care of it, and, well, I think it belongs to them."

"Oh, but, dear—"

"No, really. And if it does belong to me, well then, I can give it to whoever I want, right? Well, I think the crabs should have it in their library. So anyway, please, I want you to have it."

If there had been treasure buried there, Casey reasoned, it would have been found when they excavated for the library. And if it was still buried there, maybe it was better if it stayed there forever. Casey knew that the treasure itself wasn't bad but, even if he could have returned it to the ancestors of the original owners, it would probably just lead to more greed. Still, it was fun to think it could have been missed and that it was still buried, deep under the sand directly beneath the X formed by the dolphins. After all, when it comes to buried treasure, everyone knows that X marks the spot.

CPSIA information can be obtained at www.ICGtesting.com
Printed in the USA
BVOW06s0234100716

454878BV00002B/5/P